THIS WALKER BOOK BELONGS TO:

_____

_____

_____

For Philippa, Richard,
Tim and Sophie

First published 1993 by Walker Books Ltd
87 Vauxhall Walk, London SE11 5HJ

This edition published 2016

15 14 13 12

© 1993 Jez Alborough

The right of Jez Alborough to be identified as author/illustrator of this work has been asserted by him
in accordance with the Copyright, Designs and Patents Act 1988

This book has been typeset in Garamond

Printed in China

British Library Cataloguing in Publication Data:
a catalogue record for this book is available from the British Library

ISBN 978-1-4063-1074-0

www.walker.co.uk

Cuddly Dudley

JEZ ALBOROUGH

WALKER BOOKS
AND SUBSIDIARIES

LONDON • BOSTON • SYDNEY • AUCKLAND

Dudley loved to play.
He loved to play
jumping,

diving,

and splashing.
But most of all
Dudley loved to play ...

all by himself.

The trouble was, Dudley was such a lovely, cuddly penguin

that whenever his brothers and sisters found him on his own

they just couldn't resist having a huddle and a waddle and a cuddle with him.

"Go away," Dudley would say. "Leave me alone."

"We can't," came the reply. "You're just too cuddly, Dudley."

"I'm fed up with all your huddling and waddling and cuddling," said Dudley one day.

"I'm going to find a place where I can play all on my own." And off he went.

He waddled

and he toddled

for many, many miles

until,
quite by chance,

he found …

a little wooden house which looked perfect for a penguin.

And it seemed to be empty.

"At last!" said Dudley. "A house of my own – a place where I can jump about all day without being disturbed."

Just then there came a rap-tap-tap at the little wooden door.

"It's us," said two of Dudley's sisters. "We followed your waddleprints. Can we come in?"

"No, you jolly well can't," said Dudley. "I'm very busy and I don't want to be disturbed, so please go away." And he shut the little wooden door and was alone once more.

"At last!" said Dudley. "A house of my own –

a place where I can splash about all day without being…"

Just then there came a rap-tap-tap at the little wooden door.

"It's us," said his brothers and sisters. "We followed your waddleprints. Can we come in and…?"

"No, you jolly well can't," said Dudley. "I don't want to huddle and waddle and cuddle. So for the very last time … STOP FOLLOWING ME AROUND!"
He slammed the little wooden door and was alone once more.

"At last!" sighed Dudley. "A house of my own…"

BANG, BANG, BANG went the little wooden door.

"That does it," he said. "When I catch those penguins I'll…"

But it wasn't the penguins at the little wooden door. It was a great big man. "My word!" said the great big man. "What an adorable penguin!"

"Give us a cuddle!" he cried, and chased Dudley all round the house and out into the snow.

Dudley ran

and ran

and escaped from the man.

Then he decided to head back home. But which way was home?

Crunch, crunch, crunch went Dudley, looking for some waddleprints to follow. But when night came, he was still alone … and completely lost … and now, for the first time, he was lonely. He climbed a hill to get a better view, and at the top he saw …

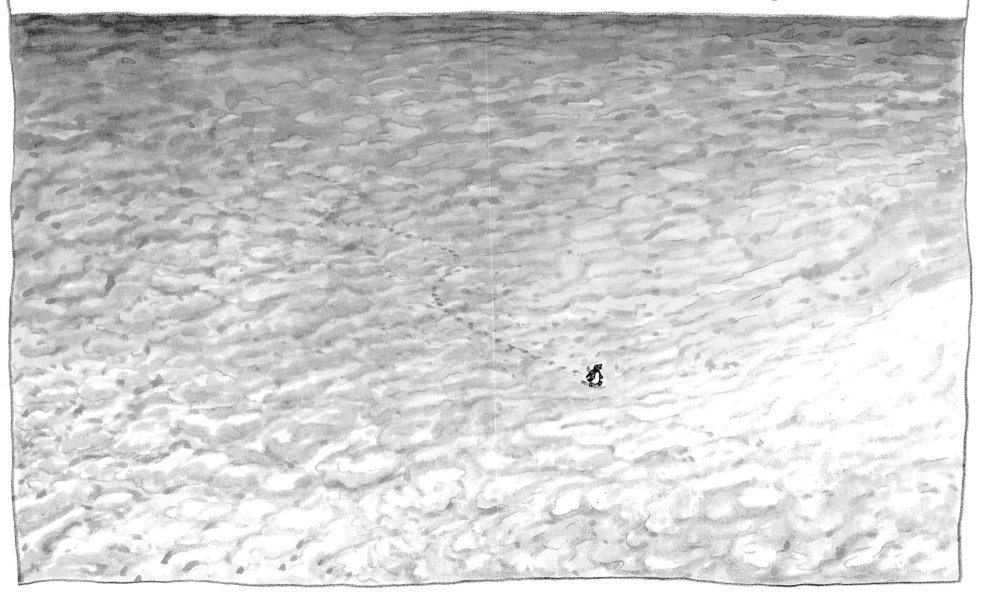

an enormous orange moon with hundreds of tiny sparkling stars huddled all around.

"Excuse me," said a penguin from the foot of the hill. "Have you finished being alone yet? Only we wondered, now that you're back ... if you wouldn't mind ... whether we could ... it's just that you're so ... *so...*"

"CUDDLY!" shouted Dudley.

And he bounced down the hill as fast as he could.

Then Dudley and all his brothers and sisters had the best huddling, waddling, cuddling session that they'd *ever* had. UNTIL …

"GIVE US A CUDDLE!"

OTHER BOOKS BY JEZ ALBOROUGH

978-1-84428-481-8

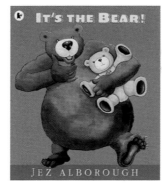
978-1-84428-475-7

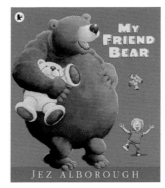
978-1-84428-479-5

978-0-7445-8273-4

978-1-4063-0173-1

978-1-4063-0456-5

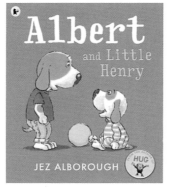
978-1-4063-5751-6

978-1-84428-457-3

978-1-4063-1076-4

JezAlborough.com

AVAILABLE FROM ALL GOOD BOOKSELLERS

WWW.WALKER.CO.UK